The Christmas Grump

CHRISTMAS
GRUMP

written and illustrated by

JOSEPH LOW

A MARGARET K. MC ELDERRY BOOK

Atheneum   1977   New York

For all dear Grumps, everywhere

Library of Congress Cataloging in Publication Data

Low, Joseph
   The Christmas grump.

  "A Margaret K. McElderry book."

  SUMMARY: A mouse resents the fact that no Christmas presents are ever placed under the tree for him.

  [1. Mice—Fiction. 2. Christmas stories] I. Title.
PZ7.L9598Ch [E]   77-3903
ISBN 0-689-50092-0

First Edition

Something about Christmas bothered Sam.
When he saw Christmas coming,
 he got more and more grumpy.
"Such a fuss about nothing!" he thought.
"Wrapping all those presents in pretty paper!

"And hiding them in the closet.
And putting all those silly things
on that silly tree.

"And all that cheerful music.
  And everyone looking so happy!
  Nobody ever gives *me* a present," he thought.

At night he knocked the presents
from the closet shelf, and the children were
scolded for it next morning.
Sam laughed. But it wasn't a happy laugh.

He scratched the Christmas record. It sounded
awful, and the children were scolded again.

On Christmas Eve he kicked the stockings
from the mantel.
And he scattered the presents all about.

He climbed into the grandfather clock
and stopped the works.

Just as he was chewing on the Christmas tree,
hoping to make it fall, he heard a noise.
He stopped chewing and listened.
It came from the chimney.

Some black boots appeared.
Then some red britches.
Then a fat, red coat.

And there stood Santa Claus!

Sam was frightened.
He hid behind the clock.

"What's this?" said Santa, looking about with
a frown. "The stockings are on the floor.
The presents have all been scattered.
And someone has been chewing at the tree!"

"We must put that right," he said.
He hung the stockings back on the mantel.
And he stacked the presents around the tree
so the chew-marks wouldn't be seen.
Then he looked around to be sure everything was
right again. And he saw Sam's mousehole.

"Goodness," said Santa. "They forgot old Sam!"
And he pulled a very small box from his pack.
He wrote Sam's name on it
and placed it right beside the hole.

Then away he went: up the chimney and gone!

Sam sidled up to the box.
He didn't know what to think.

His name was on it!
Could it be — a present of his very own?

"I must wait till morning," he said to himself.
"I'll just put it outside my hole.
 Then, when the others are opening their
 presents, I can open mine."

But he was a terribly curious mouse.
He couldn't wait. In the box he found
a bit of his favorite cheese. Some peanut
butter crackers. And four beautiful jelly beans.

Then he saw something else — something Santa
must have dropped on his way to the chimney —
a handsome pink silk coat.
He looked at it carefully.

"Too small for the children," he said.
"Much too small for the parents.
 Just about right for a mouse."
 And he tried it on. A perfect fit!

Maybe it was a magic coat.
Maybe he just felt happy that someone,
at last, had given *him* a present.
All of a sudden, Christmas seemed wonderful!

He danced about the floor,
in and out among the boxes.

He did some handsprings and somersaults.
He ran to the back of the tree, pulled off
four little sprigs, and put one on the top
of each stocking. "Good!" he said.

3

He couldn't fix the scratched record, but he
found a new one and put it on the player.
"Good," he said again.

Then he ran up the clock, put the hands where
they should have been, and started it going.
"Better," he said.

He found some ribbon and ran round and round,
weaving through the pile of presents,
making a lovely pattern.
"Best of all!" he cried.

Sam was so excited, he couldn't sleep.
So he sat up all night, playing the new
record, very softly, over and over again.
Just before morning he dozed off.

He was sound asleep, inside his hole,
when the children came down.
"Look," they cried. "What a beautiful thing Santa
did this year! Maybe he had a new helper."

And they called their mother and father,
who were still sleepy
and would rather have stayed in bed.
When their mother saw the pattern of ribbons on
the presents, she gave their father a tender look.
She thought he had done it.

"Let's play the new record," she said.
"I see it's already on the player.
  Somebody left it turned on all night — but we
  won't worry about that now."
They all sang along with the record:
  all the old carols they loved so well.

It was this that woke Sam.
He joined in the singing. He knew the words
and the tunes now, and he liked them.

"Something odd about that record," said the
father. "It seems squeaky. But never mind —
play the other side."
And so they did, and they sang again.
Sam sang a little more softly.
Everybody was happy.

Sam, in his bright new coat, was happiest of all.
"Isn't this nice," he thought.
"I'll put my new coat away in a safe place and
wear it only once a year.
I'll never be a Christmas Grump again."